LEGO CITY

ALL HANDS ON DECK!

By Marilyn Easton
Illustrated by Kenny Kiernan

SCHOLASTIC INC.

NEW YORK   TORONTO   LONDON   AUCKLAND

SYDNEY   MEXICO CITY   NEW DELHI   HONG KONG

ISBN 978-0-545-33166-1

LEGO, the LEGO logo, the Brick and Knob configurations and the Minifigure are trademarks of the LEGO Group. © 2011 The LEGO Group. Produced by Scholastic Inc. under license from the LEGO Group.

All rights reserved. Published by Scholastic Inc. SCHOLASTIC and associated logos are trademarks and/or registered trademarks of Scholastic Inc. Lexile is a registered trademark of MetaMetrics.

16

40

14 15/0

Printed in the U.S.A.
First printing, August 2011

The harbor is filled with ships.

A sailor is mopping the deck.

The captain steers the ship. He will make sure it goes where it needs to.

9

A sailor looks out at the water.
He sees a scuba diver.

He also sees a windsurfer.
The windsurfer does a cool trick.

Oh, no!
The windsurfer is heading toward some rocks!

"All hands on deck!" the captain yells.

The captain gives the sailors their orders. They will go help the windsurfer.

The sailors find the windsurfer.
They throw him a lifesaver.

"Dude! That was close," says the windsurfer.

"Next time I'll be sure to stay clear of those rocks!" says the windsurfer.